Moose
and
Magpie

by Bettina Restrepo

illustrated by Sherry Rogers

Moose lived where the willow trees touched the ground and the lily pads floated on the water.

With the exception of cows with calves, moose live alone.

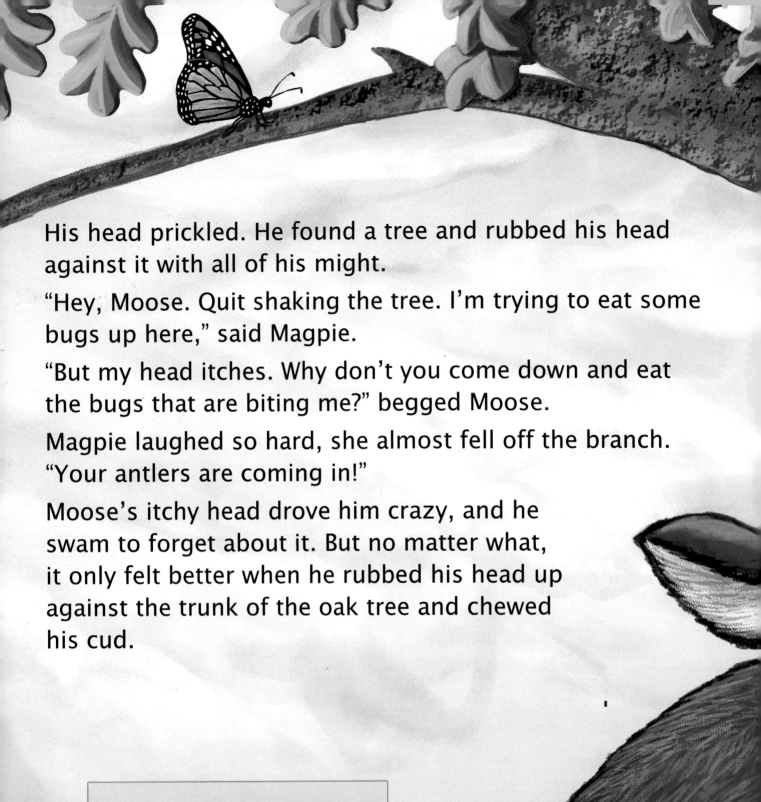

His head prickled. He found a tree and rubbed his head against it with all of his might.

"Hey, Moose. Quit shaking the tree. I'm trying to eat some bugs up here," said Magpie.

"But my head itches. Why don't you come down and eat the bugs that are biting me?" begged Moose.

Magpie laughed so hard, she almost fell off the branch. "Your antlers are coming in!"

Moose's itchy head drove him crazy, and he swam to forget about it. But no matter what, it only felt better when he rubbed his head up against the trunk of the oak tree and chewed his cud.

Cows are females. Bulls are males and grow antlers . . . an itchy process.

Magpie told him jokes to ease his mind. "What do the liberty bell and moose have in common?"

Moose didn't know much about history. "I don't know. Tell me."

"They both have bells that don't work," cackled Magpie.

The bell is the flappy part of the skin that hangs off a moose's throat. Bells can be two feet long! So far, scientists aren't sure what they are used for, although there are several different theories.

South Carolina History

California History

Discover Rocklin California

New Hampshire History

Virginia History

Pennsylvania History

Reading is Fun!

As the summer grew warmer, Moose's antlers grew big as his appetite. He ate as many leaves as he could find to fill his four stomachs.

Every day, Magpie had a new joke. "Do moose eat chocolate mousse?"

Moose thought about the question. "What kind of leaves are in it?"

Magpie shook the branch with her snickering. "Moose wouldn't eat mousse. They're herbivores."

Herbivores only eat plants.

One day, Magpie found Moose by the river to tell him a new joke. "Do moose use hair mousse?"

Moose spit water out of his mouth. "I don't even use a brush!"

Magpie settled on Moose's antlers for an easy ride through the water. "You are right! Moose have two sets of hair, and they would get too poofy."

The layer of hair closest to the moose's skin is like thermal underwear. The outer layer is hollow and acts as insulation against the cold. The hollow outer layer of hair helps the moose float while it swims.

As summer turned to fall, leaves flittered down from the trees. Magpie spent her days building a bigger nest. Moose rested under the trees. Magpie fluttered down in the evenings to look for bugs on Moose.

"Why doesn't the tooth fairy visit a moose?"

Moose had never seen a fairy, only lightning bugs. "I never answer your riddles correctly, but this time I know! Moose don't have pillows, so there is no place for the tooth fairy to look."

Moose shook his head to make Magpie fly away. She began to sing a tune.

> *The moose went over the mountain.*
> *The moose went over the mountain.*
> *The moose went over the mountain,*
>   *because it's time to go.*

"You're right. I'll feel better if I walk toward the mountains."

Moose migrate to mate.

Magpie followed him. "How do you catch a unique moose?"

Moose finally thought up an answer. "You *nique* up on him," he said.

Moose perked up his ears. "Be quiet, Magpie. I hear hunters."

Magpie whispered, "How do you catch a tame moose?"

Moose snorted and stamped his hooves at the bird. "Be quiet!"

Magpie snickered. "Tame way!"

The hunters thought they heard other humans, so they packed up and went somewhere else to hunt.

The hunters left the area because of Magpie. Some magpies can imitate human voices.

Moose felt confused and hungry. Mountains were to his right, and the river was to his left.

Moose bellowed to Magpie, "Where are we? This doesn't feel like the right place."

Magpie felt sorry for Moose. "Why did the moose cross the road?"

Moose slumped his head. "I don't know."

Magpie pointed with her wing. "He didn't cross the road. He swam in the river to that island over there."

Scientists don't know how some migrating animals know where to go. They seem to know by instinct.

Big Fishing

Big Mountains

Big Trees

Map of Places to See

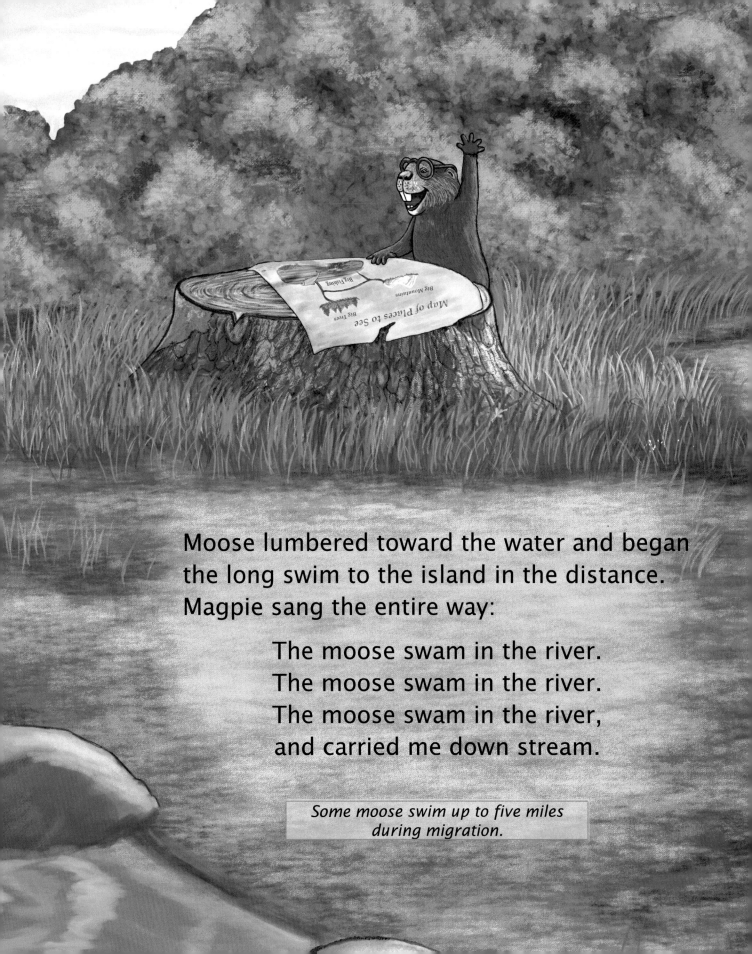

Moose lumbered toward the water and began
the long swim to the island in the distance.
Magpie sang the entire way:

> The moose swam in the river.
> The moose swam in the river.
> The moose swam in the river,
> and carried me down stream.

*Some moose swim up to five miles
during migration.*

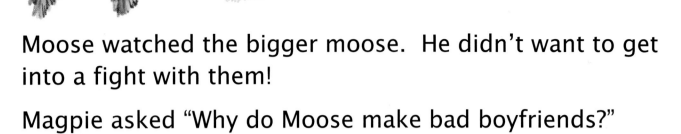

Moose watched the bigger moose. He didn't want to get into a fight with them!

Magpie asked "Why do Moose make bad boyfriends?"

"Why?"

"Because they get new girlfriends every year!"

Moose decided to return to his meadow.
Magpie sang to him all the way home.

> Bulls challenge each other for a cow's attention. The strongest bull, usually with the biggest antlers, gets the cow.
>
> Bulls don't eat as much as usual during the breeding season, which is called the rut.

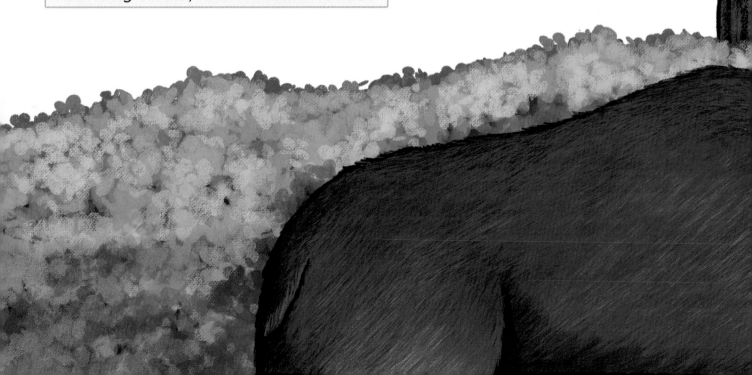

The weather was cold, and it began to snow. Moose tried to think of a riddle, but his jokes never seemed as funny as Magpie's.

Magpie called down from her nest. "Why did the moose get a ticket for littering?"

Moose went to scratch his head, but his antlers weren't there. The answer seemed clear.

"Because he dumped his antlers in the meadow!"

Antlers are made of bone. When they fall off, bugs, birds, mice, and other animals nibble on them. Deer lick the fallen antlers for extra vitamins. By spring, most antlers have disappeared or have been eaten.

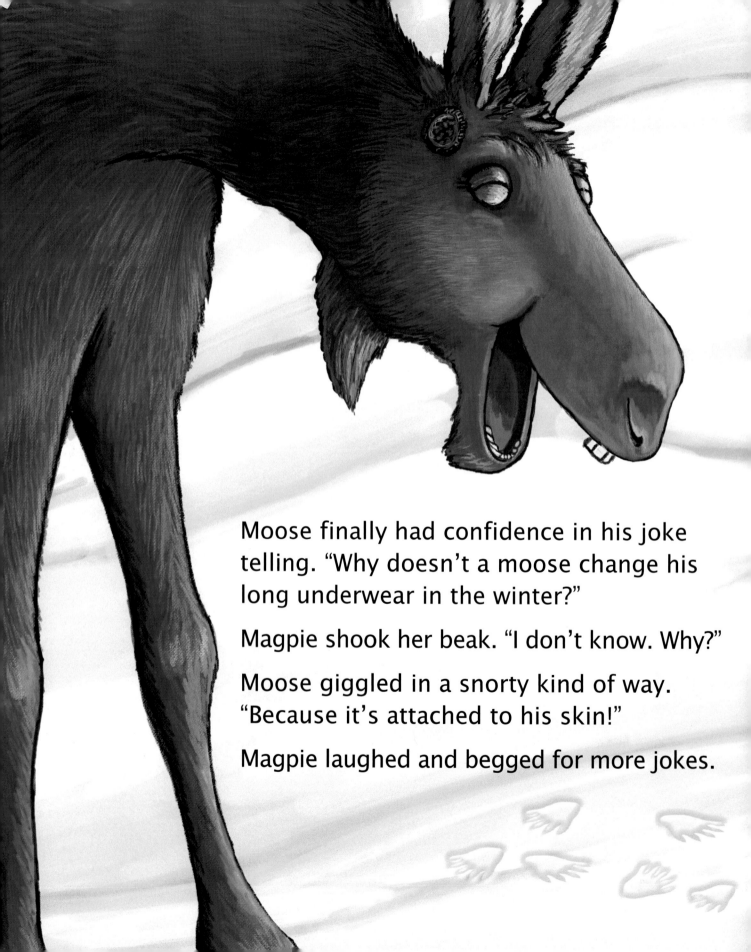

Moose finally had confidence in his joke telling. "Why doesn't a moose change his long underwear in the winter?"

Magpie shook her beak. "I don't know. Why?"

Moose giggled in a snorty kind of way. "Because it's attached to his skin!"

Magpie laughed and begged for more jokes.

Moose said, "Okay, so two
moose walked into a lodge . . ."

Is it for real? Moose and Birds

To see photos and even some videos of moose and magpies together, go to the book's links as described above.

Flies, ticks, and insects are drawn to moose. Magpies eat the bothersome creatures, making the moose more comfortable. This easy food may be why magpies and other birds are commonly seen following moose around.

However, animals don't really talk to each other like they do in this book. Nor do animals read books or use hair brushes like the illustrations show!

Magpies, however, really do gather man-made things to put in their nests! They seem to like shiny things. Sometimes they will even weave shiny things into the nest itself.

What do moose eat?

Moose spend most of their time eating. They are **herbivores**, meaning they only eat plants.

During the summer months, they eat grass, leaves, and water plants. They will even dive into the water to get the plants.

In the colder months, they eat twigs, barks and roots. They especially seem to eat willow and aspen trees. They will also eat conifer (pine) tree needles and branches.

Moose Antlers

Unlike horns, antlers grow and are shed every year.

Moose are not the only animals that grow antlers. Male deer and elk also grow antlers.

When a male calf is about six or seven months old, he will start to develop little antler buds.

When antlers first start to grow, they are covered with a soft dark fuzzy skin called velvet.

Antlers are bones that grow out of the skull. They are made from calcium, just like our bones.

By late summer, the antlers reach full size, the blood supply dries up, and the velvet drops off, leaving the whitish antlers that are so recognizable.

Between December and early February, the males' antlers fall off, and the new ones start to grow in immediately.

Match the moose body adaptation description to its body part. Answers are upside down on the bottom of the page.

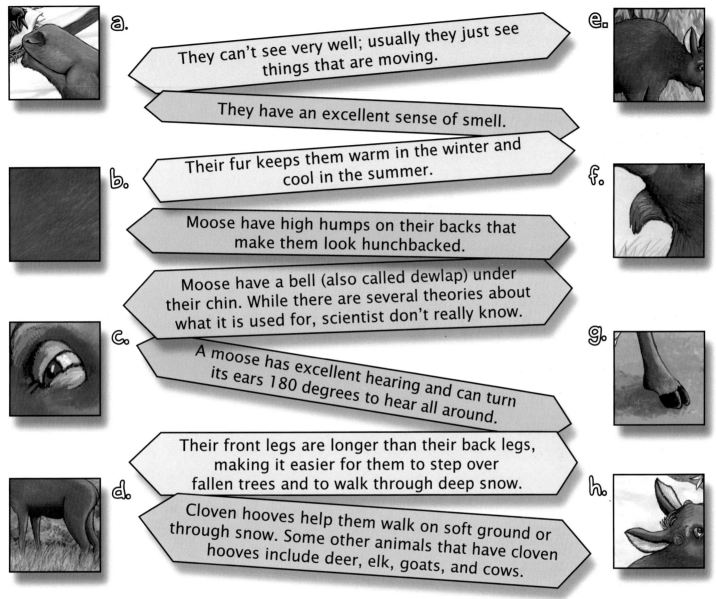

a.

They can't see very well; usually they just see things that are moving.

They have an excellent sense of smell.

Their fur keeps them warm in the winter and cool in the summer.

b.

Moose have high humps on their backs that make them look hunchbacked.

Moose have a bell (also called dewlap) under their chin. While there are several theories about what it is used for, scientist don't really know.

c.

A moose has excellent hearing and can turn its ears 180 degrees to hear all around.

Their front legs are longer than their back legs, making it easier for them to step over fallen trees and to walk through deep snow.

d.

Cloven hooves help them walk on soft ground or through snow. Some other animals that have cloven hooves include deer, elk, goats, and cows.

e.

f.

g.

h.

1c, 2a, 3b, 4e, 5f, 6h 7d, 8g

Moose Fun Facts

Moose are related to deer. In fact, they are the largest member of the deer family.

Moose are the state animals for both Alaska and Maine.

The word "moose" is both singular and plural. It comes from an Algonquin word meaning "twig eater."

Moose may migrate up and down mountains.

Moose breed from early September to late October. *What season is that?*

A cow (female moose) is usually a little over two years old when she gets pregnant for the first time.

Calves are born in May or June. They can outrun humans and swim when only a few days old. *In what season are calves born?*

Just like human mothers, cows can have twins.

Calves weigh 28 to 35 lbs. (13 to 16 kg.) when born. *How much did you weigh when you were born? How much do you weigh now? Do you now weigh more, less, or about the same as a newborn moose calf?*

Moose are mammals, like us, so the calves drink milk from their mothers. They start to eat food when they are a few days old. Calves are completely weaned off their mother's milk by fall, when she will probably get pregnant again.

By the time they are five months old, they can weigh as much as 300 lbs. (136 kg.). *Is this more or less than you weigh? By how much?*

The migration for breeding takes place in the fall. Bulls (male moose) that are at least two years old will rut or will fight to prove their strength. Generally the strongest male, or the one with the largest antlers, is considered to be the best catch as a mate.

Moose may die of diseases or by being hit by cars—especially during the rutting season.

Predators include wolves and bears—especially if moose are caught in snow that is too deep for them to move through easily. Some humans hunt moose to eat the meat and use the hides.

Half of all moose die within the first year. The moose that survive the first year can live 15 to 20 years.

Moose in Alaska are the biggest moose, and a bull may weigh up 1,600 lbs. (726 kg.).

A full-grown cow is shorter than the bull but can weigh up to 800 lbs. (363 kg.).

It is possible for a bull's antlers to grow 4 to 5 feet (1.2 to 1.5 m.) across!

A mother cow will chase the calf away when it is almost a year old. By that time, the young moose is old enough to take care of itself.

At the end of the rutting season, the moose will all return to their own wintering territories.

Cows attract bulls with their strong calls and scent.

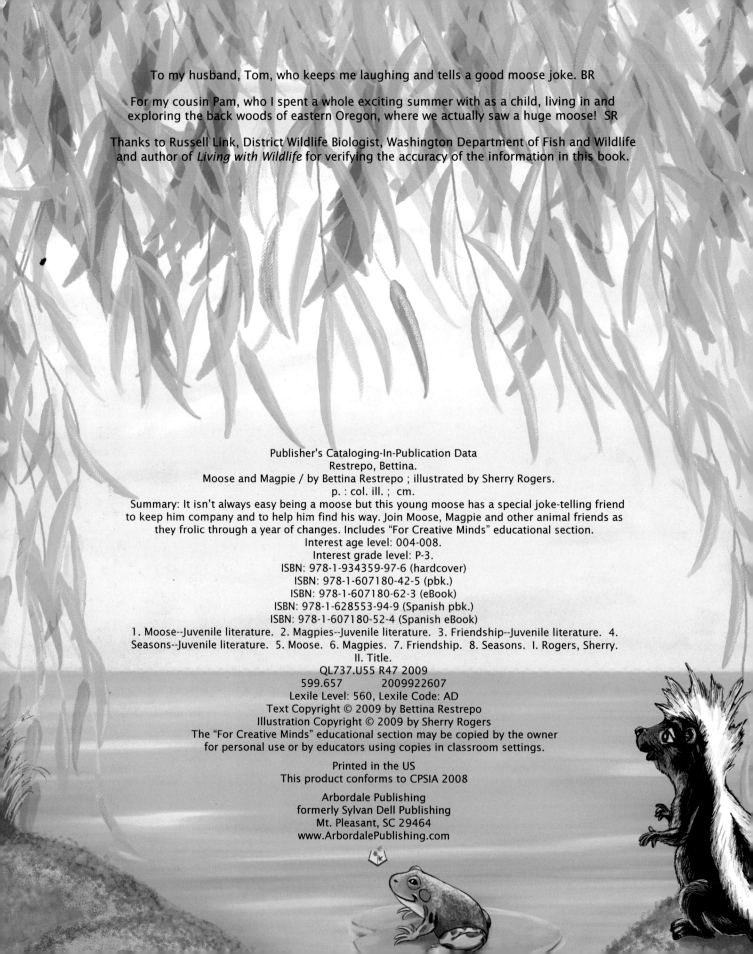

To my husband, Tom, who keeps me laughing and tells a good moose joke. BR

For my cousin Pam, who I spent a whole exciting summer with as a child, living in and exploring the back woods of eastern Oregon, where we actually saw a huge moose! SR

Thanks to Russell Link, District Wildlife Biologist, Washington Department of Fish and Wildlife and author of *Living with Wildlife* for verifying the accuracy of the information in this book.

Publisher's Cataloging-In-Publication Data

Restrepo, Bettina.
Moose and Magpie / by Bettina Restrepo ; illustrated by Sherry Rogers.
p. : col. ill. ; cm.
Summary: It isn't always easy being a moose but this young moose has a special joke-telling friend to keep him company and to help him find his way. Join Moose, Magpie and other animal friends as they frolic through a year of changes. Includes "For Creative Minds" educational section.
Interest age level: 004-008.
Interest grade level: P-3.
ISBN: 978-1-934359-97-6 (hardcover)
ISBN: 978-1-607180-42-5 (pbk.)
ISBN: 978-1-607180-62-3 (eBook)
ISBN: 978-1-628553-94-9 (Spanish pbk.)
ISBN: 978-1-607180-52-4 (Spanish eBook)
1. Moose--Juvenile literature. 2. Magpies--Juvenile literature. 3. Friendship--Juvenile literature. 4. Seasons--Juvenile literature. 5. Moose. 6. Magpies. 7. Friendship. 8. Seasons. I. Rogers, Sherry. II. Title.
QL737.U55 R47 2009
599.657   2009922607
Lexile Level: 560, Lexile Code: AD

Printed in the US
This product conforms to CPSIA 2008

Arbordale Publishing
formerly Sylvan Dell Publishing
Mt. Pleasant, SC 29464
www.ArbordalePublishing.com